LOOK AND FIND®
ICE AGE™
DAWN OF THE DINOSAURS

Illustrated by Art Mawhinney

Cover inset illustrated by Blue Sky Studios

Written by Caleb Burroughs

Ice Age: Dawn of the Dinosaurs
©2009 Twentieth Century Fox Film Corporation.
All Rights Reserved.

Published by Louis Weber, C.E.O.
Publications International, Ltd.
7373 North Cicero Avenue, Lincolnwood, Illinois 60712
Ground Floor, 59 Gloucester Place, London W1U 8JJ

Customer Service: 1-800-595-8484 or customer_service@pilbooks.com

www.pilbooks.com

Manufactured in China.

p i kids is a registered trademark of Publications International, Ltd.
Look and Find is a registered trademark of Publications International, Ltd., in the United States and in Canada.

8 7 6 5 4 3 2 1

ISBN-13: 978-1-4127-7111-5
ISBN-10: 1-4127-7111-0

Crash and Eddie have found a gleaming jewel. The trouble is, it's in the middle of a giant spiderweb! While those two escape the monster's trap, help Manny and Sid find these other precious gems.

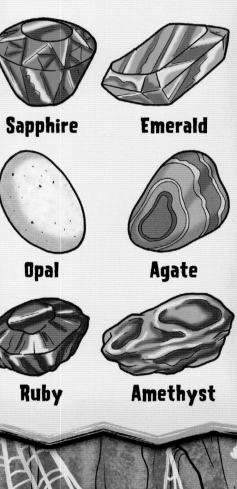

Sapphire

Emerald

Opal

Agate

Ruby

Amethyst

Manny will soon be a proud papa. Preparing for the new baby, he has built a beautiful playground. Manny's friends and neighbors have gathered to gaze at his handiwork. Look around the playground for these friends who are excited for Manny and his new family.

Eddie

Diego

Sid

Scrat

Scratte

Crash

Sid's baby dinos play on Manny's peaceful playground — and they're trashing it! Crawl through the chaos and find these other babies that are running amok.

Beaver

Start

Armadillo

Shovelmouth

Diatryma

Aardvark

Gazelle

Sid might love his new baby dinos, but their Momma loves them more. And she wants her babies back! Take cover from the rampaging mother with these hiding friends.

Scrat

Sid

Crash

Eddie

Scratte

This baby dino

Hoping to find Sid, Manny and his friends find themselves in a strange new world—a land of dinosaurs! Trek through this terrain filled with terrible lizards and find these dinosaurs.

Terry Pterodactyl

Archie Archaeopteryx

Tracy Triceratops

Pablo Pachycephalosaurus

Gary Guanlong

Sarah Sauropod

Buck to the rescue! The swashbuckling hero swings to the rescue of Manny and Diego, who are being gulped down by a carnivorous plant. While Buck saves his two friends, be on the lookout for these other fearsome flora.

Violent violet

Killer chrysanthemum

Lethal lilac

Deadly dandelion

Vicious vine

Poisonous pansy

Manny and Diego are caught in a herd of angry, stampeding headbutters. Put your heads together to help the two heroes watch out for these things that might make these headbutters charge, just like bulls.

Off Buck goes into the wild blue yonder! The brave swashbuckler has harnessed a high-flying pterodactyl in order to save Sid. See if you can spot these other flying dinosaurs in the sky.

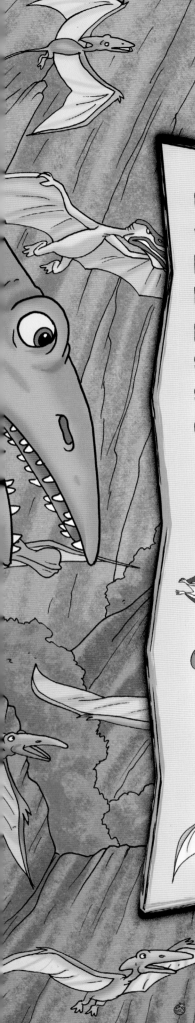

Climb back into the spider's web and help Crash and Eddie make their way through its treacherous maze.

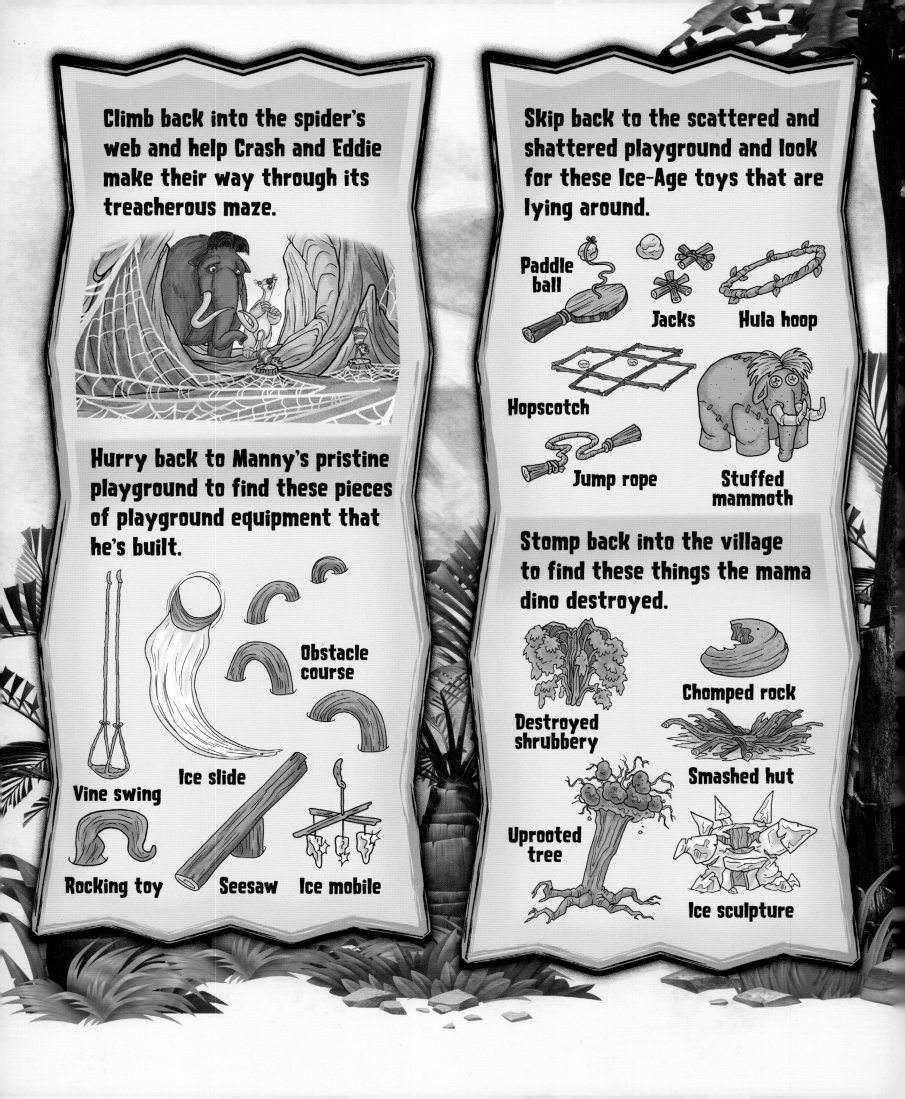

Hurry back to Manny's pristine playground to find these pieces of playground equipment that he's built.

Obstacle course

Vine swing

Ice slide

Rocking toy

Seesaw

Ice mobile

Skip back to the scattered and shattered playground and look for these Ice-Age toys that are lying around.

Paddle ball

Jacks

Hula hoop

Hopscotch

Jump rope

Stuffed mammoth

Stomp back into the village to find these things the mama dino destroyed.

Chomped rock

Destroyed shrubbery

Smashed hut

Uprooted tree

Ice sculpture

Journey back to the dawn of the dinosaurs and find these landmarks in the land of lizards.

Footprint

Watering hole

Tar pit

Hatching egg

Pterodactyl nest

Dangerous flower

Creep back through the perilous plants with Crash and Eddie to find these mouth-watering berries.

Blueberry **Strawberry** **Raspberry**

Cranberry **Mulberry** **Cherry**

Cha-cha back to the angry headbutters and find these hidden bull-fighting items.

Montera

Cape **Sword**

Trumpet **Banderilla** **Matador jacket**

Hang onto the pterodactyl with Crash and Eddie and spot 34 pieces of fruit they can use to fire at the other flyers.